This book
belongs to

....

....

GORDON'S HILL

ULFSTEAD CASTLE

FFARQUHAR STATION

TIDMOUTH SHEDS

KNAPFORD STATION

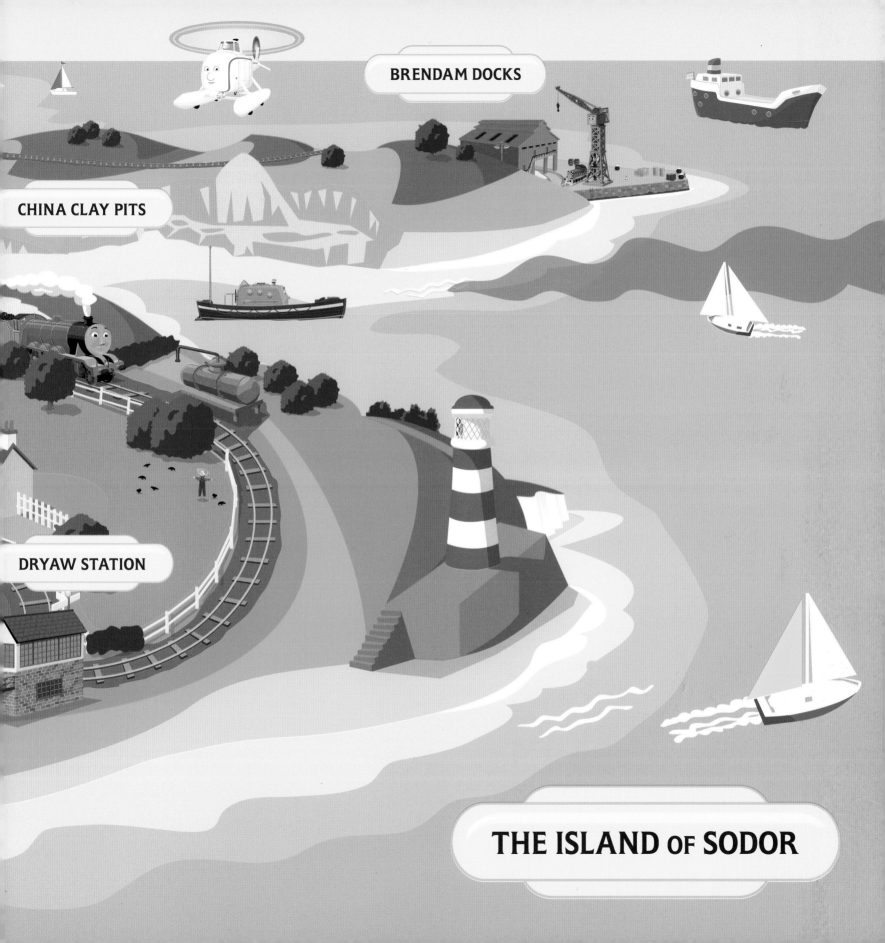

BRENDAM DOCKS

CHINA CLAY PITS

DRYAW STATION

THE ISLAND OF SODOR

EGMONT

We bring stories to life

First published in Great Britain in 2021
by Egmont Books

An imprint of HarperCollins*Publishers*
1 London Bridge Street
London SE1 9GF
www.egmontbooks.co.uk

Written by Laura Jackson
Designed by Jessica Coomber
Illustrated by Robin Davies
Map illustration by Dan Crisp

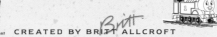

HiT entertainment   CREATED BY BRITT ALLCROFT

ISBN 978 0 7555 0049 9

71347/001

Printed in Italy

Thomas and the Robot

This is the story about Thomas the Tank Engine and some machines that came to visit ...

It was a busy day on Sodor. A Technology
Fair was taking place at Ulfstead Castle.

Inventors from all over the world were bringing
marvellous machines to the fair.
Thomas had lots to do.

"All aboard, all aboard!" Thomas sang out.
He took passengers up to Ulfstead Castle ...

... and pulled some Very Important inventions.

"Rocket booster coming through, rocket booster coming through!" puffed Thomas.

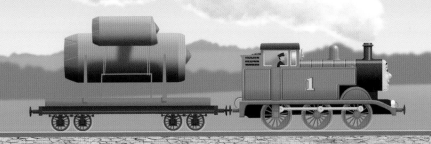

He even guided a car-plane invention to the fair.
Clickerty-clack, clickerty-clack!

When the fair finally opened, there were inventions everywhere! A huge robot called Metal Man stomped past Thomas.

Clink!

Clink!

Clink!

"Welcome to the future!" said The Fat Controller.

Thomas was excited, but he felt worried. With all these new inventions, would the Steam Team be part of the future too?

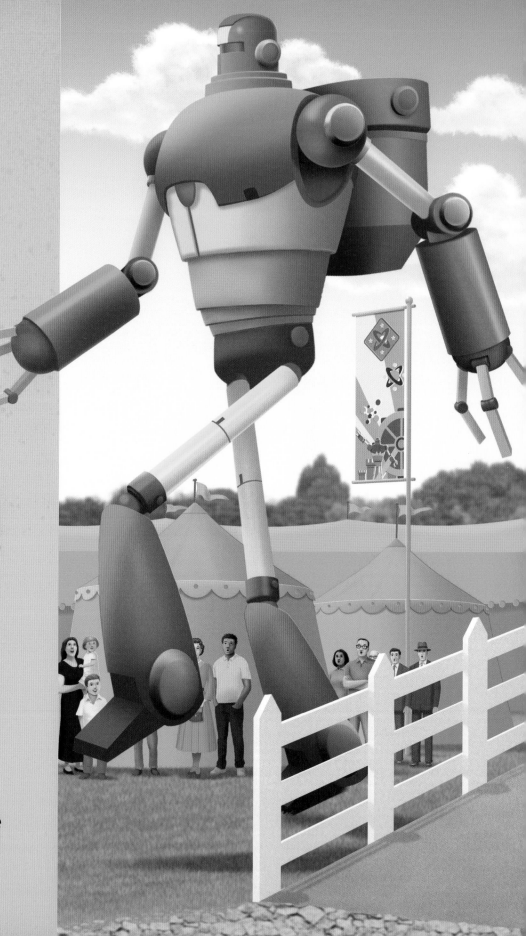

Thomas was determined to show
The Fat Controller how
useful he could be.
Just as useful as any robot.

All day long, he **chuffed** faster
than he'd ever gone before.

"Puff! Puff! Puff!"
panted poor Thomas.

At the next station, the guard was waiting on the platform.

"Watch out on the tracks today, Thomas. There's a silver machine on the rails," warned the guard.

"It's the fastest thing on Sodor!"

"It's probably another robot," Thomas sighed.

When Thomas rolled in at Ulfstead Castle, the silver machine was by the platform. It wasn't a robot at all. It was a high-speed train from Japan. **The fastest in the world!**

"**I'm Kenji,**" said the train. "You must be Thomas!"

Thomas loved meeting new friends, but he still felt worried. With robots and **faster trains**, would The Fat Controller want to replace him?

"Thomas, look!"
giggled Kenji.
A flying car buzzed
right over Thomas.

Buzz! Buzz!

Further down the
platform, Thomas
didn't notice two men
carrying the box of plans.
As the men started to
climb into Kenji's cab,
The Fat Controller
let out a shout.

"Thieves!" he cried.
"Those men have stolen
the blueprints for the
flying car!"

"Thomas, **help**!" Kenji shouted.
But it was too late. The thieves shot off
down the track in Kenji.

Whoosh!

Thomas knew he could never catch up with the fastest train in the world by himself. But he had an idea, and he needed the help of the machines …

Thomas coupled up to the rocket booster and …

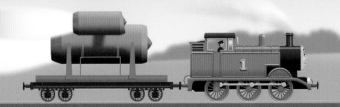

"Must catch up, must catch up!" Thomas puffed.

Thomas was uncoupled from the rocket truck and overtook Kenji.

… and all at once, Thomas was in front of Kenji!

WHOOSH! The rocket roared into life and pushed Thomas *faster, faster, faster.*

Whirr! Whirr! Whirr!
Sparks fizzed from Thomas' wheels.

The Signalperson changed the points ...

Screech! Kenji ground to a stop.

Quick as a flash, the thieves escaped with the plans.

"They've got away!" puffed Thomas. "Hang on ... what's that noise?"

Clink! Clink! Clink!

It was Metal Man and The Fat Controller! The giant robot was holding the thieves up in the air.

"Thomas and the robot **saved the day**!" said Kenji.

"The machines are much **stronger and faster** than me," said Thomas. "Maybe they are the future of Sodor ..."

"Oh no, I'd never replace my engines," said The Fat Controller.

"Steam engines are the **greatest invention** of all time!" he added.

Thomas blushed from boiler to buffer.
He didn't need to worry about robots or faster trains.
Sodor would always need the Steam Team,
but Thomas had to admit ...

... robots could be Really Useful too!

Peep!

Peep!

GORDON'S HILL

ULFSTEAD CASTLE

FFARQUHAR STATION

TIDMOUTH SHEDS

KNAPFORD STATION

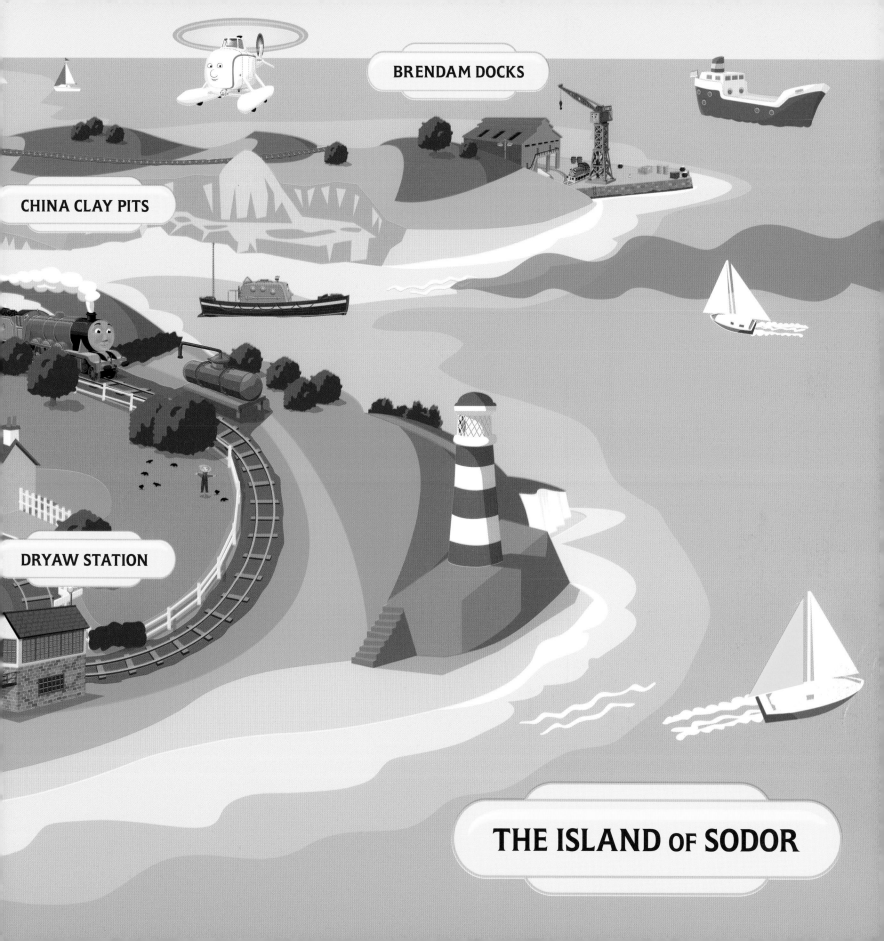

BRENDAM DOCKS

CHINA CLAY PITS

DRYAW STATION

THE ISLAND OF SODOR

The Reverend W. Awdry was the creator of 26 little books about Thomas and his famous engine friends, the first being published in 1945. The stories came about when the Reverend's two-year-old son Christopher was ill in bed with the measles. Awdry invented stories to amuse him, which Christopher then asked to hear time and time again. And now for 75 years, children all around the world have been asking to hear these stories about Thomas, Edward, Gordon, James and the many other Really Useful Engines.

The Three Railway Engines, first published in 1945.

The Reverend Awdry with some of his readers at a model railway exhibition.

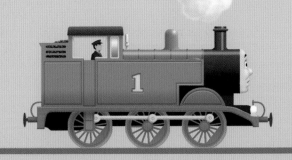